VEILED VERSES

LET'S FALL IN LOVE

VARUN KESARIA

Copyright © Varun Kesaria
All Rights Reserved.

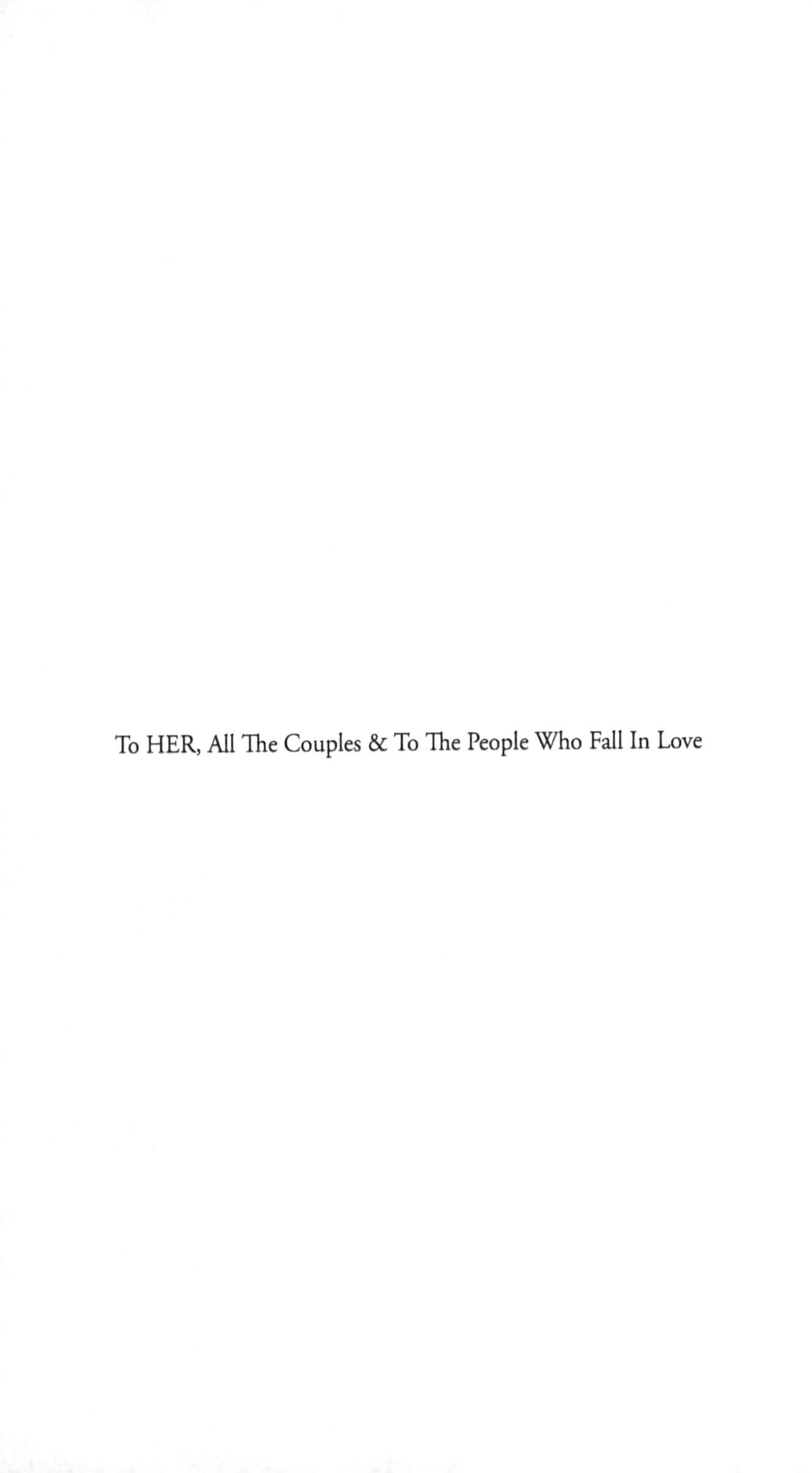

To HER, All The Couples & To The People Who Fall In Love

Contents

Preface   *vii*

Acknowledgements   *ix*

Foreword   *xi*

Prologue   *xiii*

1. Belle & Beau   1
2. Pretty Changes   2
3. In You   3
4. Yes   4
5. Fluttering Heart   5
6. My Angel   7
7. Be My Essence   9
8. Be My Life   10
9. Fairy Tale   11
10. Wanna Be With You   12
11. My Girl   15
12. My Best Half   16
13. Lovely Us   18
14. Forever You   19
15. Friend Like You   20
16. Always You   22
17. Soulfully Yours   23
18. Day 366   24
19. Meant To Be With You   26
20. Blended & Blessed   28

Contents

21. The Love - Was Never Gone — 30

22. We Stayed — 32

23. Happily Ever After — 33

24. Pretty Us — 34

25. Good Morning — 35

26. Lovely Day — 36

27. By My Side — 37

28. Pretty Pair — 38

29. Yours Own — 39

30. Two Of A Kind — 40

Epilogue — 41

Preface

This book is the result of late night thoughts and rushed up feelings. Each and every poem has a new and different story to tell. The ecstacy you will feel while reading each and every verse, each and every line, will take you to a different world of fairy tale.

This book is combination of words and lines nurtured with feelings, battled with thoughts and ceased up being the words of my heart. Nights & Days of love, ecstasy & thoughts of HER curated this book. This book, I can say, is no less than a child, who is born and brought up with immense love and care & the bond which is between ME & HER.

This book won't be possible if I got remained stucked in the chaining talks and thoughts of some people that, "No one's gonna purchase and poetry book - it will be waste of money to publish such books."

But keeping faith on the readers out there who fascinates the poetry and faith on the love with which I wrote all the poems - the result that faith is this book - Veiled Verses.

Acknowledgements

Thanks to HER & My Friends who helped me to never let down when I was about to stop writing. Just wanna let you know that - You're a part of my heart & book.

Thanks to all the readers of this book who showed love by reading the verses filled and written with love. This book won't be possible without you guys. Lot's of love, wishes, hugs & kisses.

Last but not the least, thanks to the publication house for curating and publishing this Lovely Wonder.

Foreword

Happy Reading !

Prologue

Thoughts of yours,
Flaunts my pen & Melts my heart;
Inking the lines & Thinking about you,
It makes me create a poetic art.

- Varun Kesaria

1. Belle & Beau

With red roses and diamond ring,

Holding your hands, I will be standing in front of you;

Under the starry sky I will be on my knee,

Give me a chance to love, tease and bring gifts for you;

Accept my proposal and be my proposee,

Be my belle and let me be your beau;

I will always be by your side, you have my word;

Let me share whole of my life, wardrobe and food with you.

2. Pretty Changes

I don't know why;
My cheeks go red
& My eyebrows go high;
My heart beats fast
& There's a sparkle in my eyes;
All the beautiful things happen,
At every damn time I see you smile.

3. In You

In your lap, I find peace;
In your arms, I feel calm;
Holding your hands, I get relaxed;
Oh dear, I see my whole life in you.

In your eyes, I find love;
In your hugs & kisses, I get turned on;
Seeing your smile, I find happiness;
Oh dear, I see better me in you.

In your scolding, I found care;
In your teasing, I feel fun;
Handling your mood swings, I see the childish you;
Oh dear, I feel alive when I am with you.

4. Yes

With your "Yes" to my "Will you be mine ?",
I became yours and you became mine.

With your "Me too" to my "I love you",
I took an oath to be with you.

No matter what the situations are,
You will find me always by your side;
Will always be yours truly,
I will never leave you alone,
Holding your hands firmly.

With your "Yes" to my "Will you marry me ?",
Happiness greeted me,
Excitement filled me up,
And on my face there was a big smile.

5. Fluttering Heart

Words, phrases, clauses, idioms,
Falls short for me to describe you;
A single sight of yours got me kilig,
I get smitten by the mention of yours.

I love you with my heart and soul,
You're the one and only whom I want as a whole;
I have fallen head over heels in love with you,
Come what may, holding your hand I will always be with you.

We are a match made in heaven,
Even the gods and goddesses feels our bond;
At the very damn moment I see you smile,
It takes my breath away and melts my heart.

At the very dawn of the day,
You're like breath of fresh air;
At the very dusk you flutter my heart,
With your love, affection and care.

Tease me up or get angry on me,
No matter how hard the mood swings are;
I will neither lose you nor the love for you,

Made for each other, we're never apart.

6. My Angel

There's a person who matters to me,
Matters to me a lot;
To whom I love, to whom I care for,
There's a person who excites me a lot.

There's a person who fights with me,
Who steals my food and scolds me a lot;
Yet, loves me a lot, hugs me a lot,
There's a person who praises me a lot.

There's a person who teases me,
Who makes my fun and pokes me a lot;
Yet, asks me "How was my day ?",
There's a person who cares for me a lot.

There's a person who says anything to me,
Whether it be a talk or be a abuse;
Yet, cares whether I had dinner or not,
There's a person who wishes me good night and kisses me a
lot.

There's a person to whom I wanna say,
"I am damn lucky to have you";

There's a person who makes my day,
With whom I wanna live and I wanna stay.

7. Be My Essence

Be my essence, let me be your flower;
Let the world see, the beauty of ours.

Let's spread the fragrance,
Of our love & bond,
Of your hugs & kisses,
Of my cuddles & teasings.

Let's show the World,
How we live & how we care;
How we grow & how beautiful we are.

Together forever and never apart,
Be my essence and let me be your flower.

8. Be My Life

Be my sun to which I pray,
Which wakes me up & makes my day;

Be my moon full of glare,
Which wishes me night & sweet dreams to stare;

Be my life to which I live,
In which you are present & never gonna leave.

9. Fairy Tale

Shivering words and trembling toes,
Shaking hands and murmuring thoughts;
It will be in our 70s and 80s, this things will take over;
Still you will find me by your side,
Teasing you and holding your hands beside;
Walking, talking, laughing together;
Creating a beautiful fairy tale, being yours forever.

10. Wanna Be With You

From morning till night,
From dawn till dusk,
I wanna be with you.

From your toughest hours
Till your sweetest days;
From your Happiest mornings
Till your sleepless nights,
I wanna be with you.

From Being your biggest support in your bad times,
Till being the reason of your good Times;
In your sadness and in your happiness,
I wanna be with you.

From being your best friend,
Till being your teasing person;
From being your cooking partner,
Till being your crime partner,
I wanna be with you.

I wanna hug you,
I wanna kiss you,

I wanna Marry you;
Hey...I love you;
I wanna...live with you,
I wanna be with you.

I wanna tease you,
I wanna cook for you,
I wanna shop for you;
Hey...I Miss you;
I wanna stay with you,
I wanna be with you.

I wanna travel with you,
I wanna cook for you,
I wanna click photos with you,
I wanna...wanna be with you.
I wanna Play with you,
I wanna Smile with you,
I wanna laugh with you,
I wanna be with you.

I want you happy,
I want you to smile;
Please don't be sad,
Please don't cry,
I am there for you.

I want us,
I want we,
I want happy you,
I wanna be with you.

11. My Girl

Intelligent girl with a beautiful smile,
Brilliant attitude and wings to fly;
Artist at a time and brave by soul,
She is person who is enough at sole.

Kind by heart and bright by brain,
She is the one who fears no pain.
Mighty thoughts but childish person,
She chose to try rather be in tension.

Best wishes, to the sweet girl;
Who never leaves the hope;
She wins every challenge,
And appears in the top.

Thanks to God, who created this wonder;
Who loves me a lot, I feel lucky to have her.
Thanks to God, for blessing me such a cute doll,
I just love her with my complete soul.

12. My Best Half

In my lonely days & sleepless nights, being my story tale;
In my happiest times & cheering moments,
Being the reason of my smile;
You're my everything.

Being the moon to my nights,
To which I stare and think of you;
Being the sun to my days,
Which motives me for a new day with a smile;
You're my everything.

Caring like a mother,
Scolding like a father,
Teaching like a tutor,
Supporting like a friend,
Loving like no one else can;
You're my everything.

You're my tightest hug,
You're my deepest kiss,
You're my loveliest partner,
You're my best half,
Hey, You're my everything.

From naughty talks to sweet little fights,
From morning text to late night calls;
Teasing me, Supporting me;
Scolding me, motivating me;
Caring for me;
You have always been there loving me;
You're my everything.

I am very lucky to have you,
I am very happy to be with you,
I am very eager to live my whole life with you;
Because you're my everything.

13. Lovely Us

In our life,
It's mature you & childish me;
In our daily talks,
It's humming you & talkative me;
Whenever we meet,
It's pleasing you & annoying me;
In the mood swings,
It's irritated you & calmed me;
When we're in mood,
It's playful you & naughty me;
In our outings,
It's shopoholic you & foodoholic me;
But in this beautiful world,
I am with you & You're with me;
In this heavenly bliss,
We're not different from one another;
We're the opposites :
Attracting each other,
Caring each other,
Loving each other,
For the eternity.

14. Forever You

Is it something else or is that your thought which rules my mind;

It that the blood or Is that your love which flows through my veins;

Is it the heart or is it you inside my soul which keeps me alive.

15. Friend Like You

From the rainbows to the rivers,
From the winters to the monsoon,
In the summer days and in this beautiful world;
You have always been by my side,
Keeping your comfort aside;
I am very lucky to have a friend like you.

Correcting me in my odds,
Appreciating me in my wins,
Supporting me when I lose;
That's the reason,
You being the one, every time I choose.

Loving me unconditionally,
Teasing me beautifully,
Caring me childly,
I wish everyone should have a friend like you.

Words are not enough to describe the bond we share,
Time is not enough to spend our togetherness;
Our bond is beyond all the sayings,
Our togetherness is beyond the eternity.

Thanks for being the one;
The one with whom I can share my whole life,
Including silly talks and raging heat;
The one with whom I can share my things,
Including my favorite food and favorite clothes;
Thanks for being the best fire brigade,
Thanks for being the safest locker.

Our friendship is the most beautiful feeling,
To have you in my life is the most worthy thing;
I am very lucky to have a friend like you;
I wish everyone should have a friend like you.

16. Always You

In your eyes, I see beautiful us;
In your arms, I find peace;
In your heart, I find myself;
Holding your hands, did miracles.

With you I am myself,
With you I am happy,
With you I feel safe,
With you I found a better me.

Seeing you, my heart skips a beat;
Feeling you, my heart flourishes the mood;
Touching you, my heart goes high;
Cherishing the bond, love, intimacy at whole.

17. Soulfully Yours

My hands met yours,
Your heart met mine;
Eyes filled with love,
Souls got engaged;
Hey love - let's be with eachother,
And everything will be fine.

18. Day 366

We started as a stranger,
Settled up being soulmates,
Will cease up being familiar.

From day one to day 366;
We fought,
We cried;
We suffered;
But still the journey is on.

From Who are you to How are you;
We laughed,
We enjoyed,
We loved,
And yet the happiest days are waiting ahead.

It's neither YOU nor ME,
It's always US, it's always WE;
We are two of a kind,
We fight, we fix, we stay.

No matter what the misunderstandings were,
We stayed and believed in us;

No matter what the issues will be,
We will stay and believe the bond we share.

More " This Day " are yet to come,
More days of fun & love are waiting ahead;
Let's tease, irritate, love each other,
Let's be together and embrace the life with one another.

19. Meant To Be With You

My late night tears,
My early morning smile;
All is meant to be with you.

In the chilling nights, having you by my side;
In the melting noon, scolding me aside;
Every damn thing is beautiful If it's with you.

My naughty jokes & childish talks,
My horrific laughs & teasing taunts,
All is meant to be with you.

My bubbling anger & giggling mood,
Making me smile you always stood;
Sometimes laughing & sometimes screaming,
In every odd times together we stood.

My hands to hug you,
My lips to kiss you,
My legs to tease you,
My soul to love you,
And myself to be with you;

Hey Love - Everything is meant to be with you.

20. Blended & Blessed

The day I saw her,
The heart was on roll;
Everything seemed beautiful;
Eyes craving to see her again and again.

The day I met her,
My heart skipped a beat;
The moon appeared bigger than usual;
The hours seemed Like seconds, my heart wanting to spend
some more time with her.

The day I talked with her,
Extrovert me became introvert;
I became speechless, shyness filled me up;
The first "Hi" I still remember, it can still be heard in me.

The day we fell in love,
Earth seemed to be a beautiful place;
Wanting each other lovingly;
Our heart got engaged.

I am waiting for the Day, which will be the unforgettable day;

When we will Marry each other;

When we will be able live together;

Will wake up together, will eat together;

I am waiting for the day, when We will be

"Blended & Blessed" Together.

21. The Love - Was Never Gone

I hold your hands,
To live with you, not to leave you alone;
Trust me dear,
The Love, it's still there - was never gone.

It's the same childish me,
It's the same mature you,
It's the same lovely bond;
The Love, it's still there - was never gone.

It's just that the clouds has came up,
Clouds of the blues and delusion;
Hiding the beautiful moon,
Moon of lovely bond and affection.

Soon the clouds will pass and moon will glow,
Escalating the love and care;
Let's behold each other and embrace the bond,
Creating a fairy tale, showing the World - the love was never gone.

The moon still glows for us,

The sun still shines for us;

The wind still carries our love,

The nature still feels our bond;

Trust me dear,

The Love, it's still there - was never gone.

22. We Stayed

Storms came, lightning striked;
We trembled, we got hurt;
But the hope was still crying aloud.

Things got worst, darkness ruled;
We fought, we cried;
But the souls were still calling out loud.

Hitting all the barriers,
We tried, we loved, we stayed;
This are we,
We loved and stayed for the rainbow at the end of
thunderstorm.

23. Happily Ever After

One fine morning,

The dream came true;

The sun shined bright,

As the groom found his bride.

Ignoring the phone screening,

They woke up together;

Wishing a beautiful morning,

They hugged each other.

Spreading the joy the birds flew higher,

As the god fulfilled a couple's desire.

The vibes were pinked,

Because they were beautifully linked;

Nature showered love & flower,

As the bride & groom were about to live happily ever after.

24. Pretty Us

Eyes got linked & heart was hooked,
Hands met hands & we were obsessed;
Embracing the beauty of our beatific bond,
She became my prettiest problem,
And I became her loveliest headache.

25. Good Morning

Morning happened fine,
When the sun hit sky;
My eyes structed sunshine.

She woke up in my arms,
With a calm smile on face;
Hairs entangled with sleepy yawns,
Baby voice with the childish talks.

Hand in hand with her kiss on my cheeks,
That was the morning we crave for,
That was the "Good Morning" indeed.

26. Lovely Day

I know you can't be with me every time,
But you care for me all the time;
Mornings messed up with lots of work,
Afternoon was spent with a bit of irk.

Down the day, the evening happened,
Surviving the day we were tamed;
Wait was finally about to end,
It was the time to meet & blend.

At the coffee shop we met finally,
Holding the hands we smiled out lovingly;
"How was your day", I asked you in rush,
"Not so good until I met you", you answered with blush.

Whole day was monotonous same as ever,
Until we met, laughed & giggled with each other;
Yes my love, you're the best part of my life & day,
The moment I met you, it was indeed a lovely day.

27. By My Side

From you and me,
To us and we;
The days weren't easy,
But with you by my side,
It felt so lovely.

From morning texts,
To morning hugs;
Hurdles kept coming,
But with you by my side,
It is a dream come true.

From fighting like a child,
To playing with our baby;
The route had twists & turns,
But with you by my side,
The journey was so much fun.

Together we fight,
Together we stay;
Oh love ! There will be ups & downs,
But we alongside hand in hand,
Together we will slay.

28. Pretty Pair

Oh dear girl, I owe to you,
I owe to you my love & care;
When I was at best - you showed me love,
When I was at worst -you supported me with care.

Oh my lady, you owe me too,
You to me your hugs & kisses;
When you were sad - I hugged you tight,
When you were happy - I kissed you a lot.

These are we - amazing & childish,
Sometimes spicy - sometimes sweet;
We fight with each other so that we can end it with a hug,
We tease each other so that we can cease it with a kiss.

We are like characters of a fairy tale,
Sometimes we fight sometimes we play;
Still at the end of the day we cease it love & care,
This are beautiful we - together forever & never apart.

29. Yours Own

On the swing, sit by my side,
Rest your head on my shoulders;
Don't be afraid baby, hold my hands,
My dear lady, I am always by your side.

Whether you create blunder or make wonder,
You will find me always standing by your side;
Whether I am angry or happy am I,
My arms will be present to hug you tight, keeping the grudges aside.

Pardon my lady if I have ever let you down,
I never meant to hurt you & bring your mood down;
I just want you to know that you're never alone,
Be it a dusk or dawn, I am happily yours own.

30. Two Of A Kind

Two pretty souls sharing one single bond,
Two cute persons sharing one awesome ceremony,
Two pure heart sharing one adventurous life,
Tackling twists & turns; caring, loving, teasing each other,
Two beautiful smile sharing one amazing reason.

Epilogue

In the world of SMS you're my long paragraphed message - Full of love & care.

- Varun Kesaria